HARRY HUGGER AND THE DELIGHTFUL DAY

Dear Oaklee,
    Welcome to the world.
I hope you enjoy Harry's
story.
        Huge Hugs!

Mike Mulhall

Harry and his younger sister Harriet lived in a tall tree.

Harry liked going to school. He woke up early, brushed his teeth, combed his hair and ate a big breakfast.

Wearing a bow tie let people know that
Harry was an extraordinary hairy hamster.

Harry had a special talent. Harry was a huge hugger.

In the morning – Harry hugged his tiny merry Mom and his big daring Dad.

In the front yard - Harry hugged Harriet wonderfully well.

On the bus – Harry hugged his hug-fantastic friends.

At school - Harry hugged his
talkative teacher.

At lunch – Harry hugged his friends who'd had dreadful days.

At soccer - Harry hugged everyone who made powerful plays.

When visiting grandparents – Harry hugged his grinning grandma and his goofy grandpa.

Before bedtime – Harry hugged everyone in his fun family.

Every day, Harry spread hugging happiness.

One morning merry Mom told Harry that he could no longer give happiness hugs.

An invisible germ had come to town and it made people silly sick.

The germ moved from person to person by the tiniest touch.

For the entire spring Harry could only hug his family in their tall tree.

Every day was hard. He could not go to school, he could not play soccer, he certainly could not visit grinning grandma and goofy grandpa.

Every day Harry hugged Harriet, merry Mom and daring Dad, but he stayed away from all his fine friends.

As summer came, the germ began to lightly leave. Harry could visit his friends and play but still, there could be no happiness hugs. Harry knew his friends and family needed those helpful hugs.

One day Harry's Mom told him that doctors had chased the germ away. That was a delightful day.

Hugging was once again OK. Harry knew just what to do. He headed out wearing his best bowtie.

That day, Harry hugged all of his friends. Harry hugged grandma and grandpa. Harry hugged his teammates. Harry hugged his talkative teacher.

At the end of the delightful day, Harry and his family had a great group hug. Harry, Harriet, Mom and Dad wrapped their arms around each other and squeezed tightly. It was the best way to end a delightful day.

Lying in bed with the lights out, Harry hugged himself. Harry had been brave and strong, even when hugging was weirdly wrong.

Harry slept soundly knowing that tomorrow would be another delightful day.

---The Beginning---

Made in the USA
Columbia, SC
08 August 2020

15058137R00018